Heinrich Heine

FROM THE MEMOIRS OF
HERR VON SCHNABELEWOPSKI

GERMAN CLASSICS

Heinrich Heine

FROM THE MEMOIRS OF HERR VON SCHNABELEWOPSKI

MONDIAL

Mondial
New York

Heinrich Heine:
From the Memoirs of Herr von Schnabelewopski

German original title:
Aus den Memoiren des Herren von Schnabelewopski

Translated by Charles Godfrey Leland
and Hans Breitmann (1891)

Footnotes by Charles Godfrey Leland

Editor (2008): Andrew Moore (A.M.)

Cover image: Old view of Hamburg, between 1900 and 1914.
Photochrom print (color photo lithograph).
Source: http://commons.wikimedia.org/wiki/
image:Hamburg_Jungfernstieg_(1890-1900).jpg

ISBN 978-1-59569-102-6
Library of Congress Control Number: 2008934504

www.mondialbooks.com

CHAPTER I

My father was named Schnabelewopski, my mother Schnabelewopska. I was born as legitimate son of both, the 1st of April 1795, in Schnabelewops. My great aunt, the old lady von Pipitzka, nursed me as a child, and told me pretty tales, and often sang me to sleep with a song of which I have forgotten both the words and tune; but I can never forget the strange, mysterious way in which she nodded as she sang, and how mournfully her only tooth, the solitary hermit of her mouth, peeped out. And I can remember, too, much about the parrot, whose death she so bitterly bewailed. My old great aunt is dead now herself, and I am the only one in the world who still thinks of her parrot. Our cat was called Mimi, and our dog Joli. He had a great knowledge of human nature, and always got out of the way when I took down my whip. One morning our servant said that the dog kept his tail rather close between his legs and let his tongue hang out much more than usual, for which reason poor Joli was thrown, with some stones which were tied to his neck, into the water; on which occasion he was drowned. Our footman was called Prrschtzztwitsch. To pronounce this name properly one must sneeze at the same time. Our maid was called Swurtszska, which indeed sounds rather roughly in German, but which is musical to the last degree in Polish. She was a stout, low-built person, with white hair and blonde teeth. Besides these there was a pair of beautiful black eyes running about the house, which were called Seraphina. This was my beautiful, beloved cousin, and we played together in the garden, and watched the housekeeping of the ants, and caught butterflies and planted flowers. She laughed once like mad when I planted my little stockings in the earth, believing that they would grow up into a great pair of breeches for papa.

My father was the best soul in the world, and was long regarded as a very handsome man. He wore powdered hair, and behind a neatly braided little queue, which did not hang down, but was fastened with a little tortoise-shell comb to one side. His hands were of a dazzling whiteness, and I often kissed them. It seems as if I could still smell their sweet perfume, which made my eyes tingle. I loved my father dearly, and it never came into my mind that he could ever die.

My paternal grandfather was the old Herr von Schnabelewopski, and all I know of him is that he was a man, and my father was his son. My maternal grandfather was the old Herr von Wlrssrnski (sneeze again to pronounce this name correctly), and he is painted in a scarlet velvet coat, with a long sword, and my mother often told me that *he* had a friend who wore a green silk coat, rose-silk breeches, and white silk stockings, who swung his little chapeau-bas here and there in a rage when he spoke of the King of Prussia.

My mother, Lady von Schnabelewopska, gave me as I grew up a good education. She had read much: before my birth she read Plutarch almost exclusively, and was probably deeply impressed by one of his great men, perhaps one of the Gracchi. Hence my mystical yearning to realise the agrarian law in a modern form. My deep sympathy for freedom and equality is probably due to these maternal pre-lectures. Had she read the life of Cartouche I had possibly become a great banker.[1] How often as a boy did I play truant from school to reflect on the beautiful meadows of Schnabelewopska how to benefit all mankind. For this I was often well scolded and punished as an idler, and so had to suffer with grief and pain for my schemes for benefiting the world. The neighbourhood of Schnabelewops is, I may

---

1 Cartouche. A famous French thief whose life has long been a popular chap-book.

mention, very beautiful. There is a little river running there in which one can bathe in the summertime very agreeably, and there are the most delightful birds' nests in the copses along the banks. Old Gnesen, the former capital of Poland, is only three miles distant. There, in the cathedral, Saint Adalbert is buried. There is his silver sarcophagus, on which lies his very image, the size of life, with bishop's mitre and crosier, the hands piously folded—and all of molten silver! How often have I thought of thee, thou silver saint! Ah, how often my thoughts go back to Poland, and I stand once more in the cathedral of Gnesen, leaning on the column by the grave of Adalbert! Then the organ peals once more, as if the organist were trying a piece from Allegri's Miserere; a mass is being murmured in a distant chapel, the last rays of the sun shine through the many-coloured glass windows, the church is empty, only there lies before the silver shrine a praying figure—a woman of wondrous beauty—who casts at me a sudden side glance, which she turns as suddenly again towards the saint, and murmurs with yearning, cunning lips, "I pray to *thee!*"

In the instant in which I heard those words, the sacristan rang his bell in the distance, the organ pealed as with extreme haste like a rising tide, the beautiful woman rose from the steps of the altar, cast her veil over her blushing face, and left the cathedral.

"I pray to thee!" Were these words addressed to me or to the silver Adalbert? Truly she had turned to him, but only her face. What was the meaning of that side-glance which she first threw at *me*, whose rays flashed over my soul like a long ray of light which the moon pours over a midnight sea when it breaks from a dark cloud, and in an instant is seen no more? In my soul, which was dark as such a sea, that gleam of light woke all the wild forms which lurk in the abyss, and the maddest sharks and sword-fish of passion darted upward and tumbled together, and bit one another in the tails for ecstasy, and over it all the organ roared and stormed more terribly, like a great tempest on the Northern Sea.

The next day I left Poland.

CHAPTER II

My mother packed my trunk herself. With every shirt she put in a bit of moral advice. In after times the washerwomen got away with all my shirts, and morals too. My father was deeply moved, and gave me a long slip of paper, on which he had written out, precept by precept, how I was to behave in the world. The first article announced that I was to turn every ducat ten times before I spent it. I followed this advice at first; after a while the constant turning became tiresome. With every item of advice I received a ducat. Then he took scissors, cut the queue from his dear head, and gave it to me for a souvenir. I have it yet, and never fail to weep when I see the powdered delicate hair.

The night before I left I had the following dream: —

I wandered alone in a cheerful, beautiful place by the sea-side. It was noon, and the sun shone on the water, which sparkled like diamonds. Here and there on the beach grew a great aloe, which lifted its green arms, as if imploring, to the sunny heaven. There stood a weeping willow with its long hanging tresses, which rose and fell as the waves came playing up, so that it looked like a young water-spirit letting down her green locks, or raising them to hear the better what the wooing sprites of the air were whispering to her. And, indeed, it often sounded like sighs and tender murmurs. The sea gleamed more beautifully and tenderly, the waves rang more musically, and on the rustling, glittering waves rose the holy Adalbert, as I had seen him in the Gnesen Cathedral, with the silver crosier in his silver hand, the silver mitre on his silver head, and he beckoned to me with his hand, and nodded to me with his head, and at last, as he stood before me, he cried with an unearthly silver voice —

Yes; but I could not hear the words for the rustling of the waves. I believe, however, that my silver rival mocked me, for I stood a long time on the strand, and wept till the twilight came, and heaven and earth became sad and pale, and mournful beyond all measure. Then the flood rose — aloe and willow cracked and were wafted away by the waves, which ran back many times in haste, and came bursting up ever more wildly, rolling and embracing terribly in snow-white half rings. But then I began to perceive a noise in measured time, like the beat of oars, and there came a boat driven along by the waves. In it sat four white forms, with sallow, corpse faces, wrapped in shrouds, rowing with energy. In the midst stood a pale but infinitely beautiful woman, infinitely lovely and delicate, as if made from lily-perfume, and she sprang ashore. The boat with its spectral row-men shot like an arrow back into the rising sea, and in my arms lay Panna Jadviga, who wept and laughed, "I pray to thee!" [1]

---

1 The unexpected ending of this chapter referring to a beautiful woman and death, in a mysterious, uncanny manner, is a *tour de force* which Heine employs several times in the Reisebilder. — *Translator.*

CHAPTER III

MY first flight after leaving Schnabelewops was towards Germany, and, indeed, to Hamburg, where I remained six months, instead of going directly to Leyden and applying myself, as my parents wished, to the study of theology. I must confess that during that half-year I was much more occupied with worldly than with heavenly affairs.

Hamburg is a good city, all of solid, respectable houses. It is not the infamous Macbeth who governs here, but Banko.[1] The spirit of Banko rules and pervades this little free city, whose visible head is a high and well-wise Senate.[2] In fact it is a free state, and we find in it the greatest political freedom. The citizens can do what they please, and the high and well-wise Senate acts as it likes. Every one is lord of his own deeds—it is a true republic. If Lafayette had not been so fortunate as to find Louis Philippe he would certainly have recommended the Senate and supervisors of Hamburg to his French fellow-citizens. Hamburg is the best republic. Its manners are English, and

---

1 Of course Banquo. Pun on bank.

2 *Ein hoher und wohlweiser Senat.* A formal expression often applied officially to such bodies.

its cookery is heavenly.[1] There are, in sober truth, between the Wandrahmen and the Dreckwall, dishes to be found of which our philosophers have no conception. The Hamburgers are good people who enjoy good eating. They are much divided as regards religion, politics, and science, but they are all beautifully agreed as to cooking. Their theologians may quarrel as much as they like over the Lord's Supper, but there is no difference as to the daily dinner. Though there be among the Jews there one division who give grace or the prayer at table in German, while others chant it in Hebrew, they both eat heartily and agree heartily as to what is on the table, and judge its merits with unfailing wisdom. The lawyers, the turnspits of the law, who turn and twist it till at last they get a roast for themselves, may dispute as to whether feeing and pleading shall be publicly conducted or not, but they are all one as to the merits of feeding, and every one of them has his own favourite dish. The army is naturally of Spartan bravery, but it will not hear of black broth. The physicians vary much in treating disorders, and cure the national illness — indigestion — as Brownists, by giving still greater helpings of dried beef; or, as homeopa-

---

1 Seine *Sitten sind Englisch, und sein Essen ist himmlisch. Englisch* has the double meaning of English and angelic.

thists, by administering 1/10,000 of a drop of ab-sinthe in a great tureen of mock-turtle soup — but all practise alike when it comes to discussing the soup and the smoked beef themselves. Of this last dish Hamburg is the paternal city, and boasts of it as Mainz boasts of John Faust, or Eisleben of Martin Luther. But what is the art of printing or the Reformation compared to smoked beef! There are two parties in Germany who are at variance as to whether the latter have done good or harm, but the most zealous Jesuits are united in declaring that smoked beef[1] is a good invention, wholesome for humanity.

Hamburg was founded by Charles the Great, and is inhabited by eighty thousand small people, none of whom would change with the great man who now lies buried in Aix la Chapelle. The population of the city may amount to one hundred thousand, I am not quite sure, though I walked whole days in its streets to look at the people. It is very possible that many men escaped my attention, as I was particularly occupied with looking at the women. The latter I found were by no means lean; on the contrary, they were generally corpulent, and now and then charmingly beautiful — on the whole, of a nourishing,

---

1 *Rauchfleisch, i.e.,* smoked meat, generally known in the United States as smoked, or, more commonly, dried beef.

sensuous quality, which, by Venus! did not displease me. If they do not manifest much wild and dreamy idealism in romantic love, and have little conception of the grand passion of the heart, it is not so much their fault as that of Cupid, who often aims at them his sharpest arrows, but from mischief or unskilfulness shoots too low, and instead of the heart hits them in the stomach. As for the men, I saw among them mostly short figures, calmly reasoning cold glances, low foreheads, carelessly heavy hanging red cheeks, the eating apparatus being remarkably well developed, the hat as if nailed to the head, and the hands in both breeches' pockets, as though their owner would say, "How much must I pay, then?"

Among the lions of Hamburg we find—

1. The old Council House, or Town Hall, where the great Hamburg bankers are chiselled out of stone, and stand counterfeited with sceptres and globes of empire in their hands.

2. The Exchange, where the sons of Hammonia assemble every day, as did the Romans of old in the Forum, and where there hangs overhead a black tablet of honour, with the names of distinguished fellow-citizens.[1]

---

1 A satirical reference to a black-board hung in the Exchange, bearing the names of fraudulent or absconding members of the association.

3. The Beautiful Marianne, an extremely handsome woman, on whom the tooth of Time has gnawed for twenty years. By the way, "tooth of time" is a bad metaphor, for Time is so old that by this time he cannot have a tooth left, while Marianne has all of hers, and hair on them at that.

4. That which was once the Central Treasury.

5. Altona.

6. The original manuscripts of Marr's Tragedies.

7. The owner of the Röding Museum.

8. The Börsenhalle or Stock Exchange.

9. The Bacchus Hall.

10. And, finally, the City Theatre.

This last deserves to be specially praised. Its members are all good citizens, honourable fathers of families, who never let themselves be substituted or disguised,[1] and never act so as to deceive anybody for an instant—men who make of the theatre a church, since they convince the unhappy man who has lost faith in humanity, in the most actual manner possible, that all things in this world are not delusion and a counterfeit.[2] In enumerating the remarkable things in Ham-

---

1 *Verstellen.* To misplace, sham, disguise.

2 By all this Heine simply means that nobody is "taken in" by the acting in question.

burg, I cannot refrain from mentioning that in my time the Hall of Apollo, on the Drehbahn, was a very brilliant place. Now it has very much come down, and philharmonic concerts, and shows by professors of legerdemain, are there given, and professors of natural history are fed. Once it was different. The trumpets pealed, the drums rattled and rolled loudly, ostrich feathers fluttered, and Heloise and Minka ran the races of the Oginski polonaise, and everything was so perfectly respectable! Sweet time it was for me when fortune smiled. And this *fortune* was called Heloise. She was a charming, loving, pleasure-giving treasure, with rosy lips, a little lily nose, warm, perfumed carnation lips, and eyes like blue mountain lakes, albeit there was something of stupidity on her brow, which hung there like a gloomy cloud over a brilliant spring landscape. She was slender as a poplar, lively as a dove, with a skin delicate as an infant's. Sweet time when Fortune ever smiled on me! Minka did not laugh so much, not having such beautiful teeth; but her tears were all the lovelier when she wept, which she did on all occasions for suffering humanity; and she was benevolent beyond belief. She gave the poor her last penny — yes, for charity's sake, I have known her to be reduced to the last shift. She was so good that she refused nothing to anybody, save that which was indeed beyond her gift. This soft and yielding character contrasted charmingly with her personal appearance, which was that of a brave Juno — a bold, white neck, shaded by wild black ringlets, like voluptuous snakes; eyes which flashed forth as if ruling the world from under glooming arches of victory; purple, proud, high-curving lips; marble white commanding hands, somewhat pimpled; and she had on her right side a mother-mark in the form of a small dagger.

If I have brought you into so-called bad company, dear reader, console yourself with the reflection that it does not cost you so much as it did me. However, there will be no want, further on in this book, of ideal women — and just here I will give you a specimen, just to cheer you up, of two highly decent dames, whom I learned in those days to know and honour. These were Mrs. Pieper and Mrs. Schnieper. The first was a handsome woman in full maturity, with great blackish eyes, a great white forehead, false black hair, a bold, old Roman nose, and a mouth which was a guillotine for every good name. Indeed there could be no contrivance equal to that mouth for the speedy execution and death of a reputation. There was no prolonged struggle, no long-delayed preparation, if the best of characters once got between her teeth she smiled, but that smile was the fall of the axe, and honour was decapitated and the head rolled into the bag. She was always a pattern of propriety, honour, piety, and virtue. The same may be said in celebration of Mrs. Schnieper. She was a tender woman, with a little anxious bosom, generally curtained with a mournful thin gauze or crape, light blonde hair, and clear blue eyes, which gleamed in a frightfully crafty manner out of her white face. People said you could never hear her footfall, and indeed ere you knew it she often stood close by, and then vanished as silently as she came. Her smile, too, was death to any decent reputation, but less like the fall of an axe than the poison wind of Africa, before whose breath all flowers perish; so in the breath of this woman's voice every good name perished miserably as she smiled. Also a pattern of piety, propriety, honour, and virtue.

I shall not fail to exalt many of the sons of Hammonia, nor to praise in the highest certain men who are grandly esteemed — *videlicet,* those who are rated at several million marks *banco* — but just at present I will subdue my enthusiasm, that it may after a time flame up all the higher. For I have nothing less in my mind than to raise a temple of honour to Hamburg, according to the same plan which was sketched out some ten years ago by a celebrated man of letters, who with this intention requested every Hamburger to send him a specified inventory of his virtues and talents — with one dollar, specie — as soon as possible. I have never exactly understood why this temple of honour never appeared. Some say that the undertaker, or the man of honour who kept the temple, had hardly printed from A — *Aaron* to *Abendroth* — and only got in his first quoins, before he broke down under the weight of copy or biography sent in; others say that the high and well-wise Senate, moved by excess of modesty, prevented the project altogether, since they requested this architect of his own temple of honour to be out of Hamburg with all his virtues within four-and-twenty hours. Anyhow, from some cause or other, the work was never completed; and as I have an inborn yearning to do something great in this world, and have ever striven after the impossible, therefore I have revived this vast project, and will myself manufacture a great temple of honour to Hamburg, an immortal and colossal *book,* in which I will describe without exception all its inhabitants — wherein shall appear noble traits of secret charity which were never mentioned in a newspaper, traits of such grandeur that nobody will believe a word of them, to be preceded by a magnificent portrait of myself, as I appear when I sit in the Jungfernstieg before the Swiss Pavilion, and muse over the magnificence of Hamburg. This will be the vignette of my immortal work.

CHAPTER IV

For readers who do not know Hamburg—there are such, I suppose, in China or Upper Bavaria—I must remark that the most beautiful promenade of the sons and daughters of Hammonia bears the appropriate name of Jungfernstieg,[1] and that it consists of an avenue of lime-trees, which is bounded on one side by a row of houses, and on the other by the Alster Basin, and that before the latter, and built out into the water, are two tent-like pleasant cafes, called pavilions. It is nice to sit, especially before one called the Swiss Pavilion, of a summer day, when the afternoon sun is not too hot, but only smiles gaily and pours its rays as in a fairy dream over the lindens, the houses, the people, the Alster, and the swans, who cradle themselves in it. Yes, it is nice to sit there; and even so I sat on many a summer afternoon and thought, as a young man generally does, that is to say, about nothing at all, and looked at what a young man generally looks at, that is, the girls—yes, there they fluttered along, the charming things, with

---

1 *Jungfernstieg*. The Maidens' or Virgins' Walk.

17

their winged caps, and covered baskets, containing nothing; there they tripped, the gay Vierlander maids, who provide all Hamburg with strawberries and their own milk, and whose petticoats are still much too long; there swept proudly along the beautiful merchants' daughters, with whose love one gets just so much ready money; there skipped a nurse bearing on her arm a rosy boy, whom she constantly kissed while thinking of her lover; there wandered too the priestesses of Venus Aphrodite, Hanseatic vestals, Dianas on the hunt, Naiads, Dryads, Hamydryads, and similar clergymen's daughters; and ah! there with them Minka and Heloise! How oft I sat in that pavilion fair and saw her wandering past in rose-striped gown — it cost four shillings and threepence a yard, and Mr. Seligmann gave me his word that even though washed, and that full many times, the colour would not fade. "What glorious girls!" exclaimed the virtuous youths who sat by me, I remember how a great insurance agent, who was always bedecked like a carnival ox, said, "I'd like to have one of them for breakfast, and the other for supper, just at will, and I don't think I should want any dinner that day." — "She is an angel!" cried a sea-captain, so loudly that both the damsels at a glance looked jealously at one another. I myself said nothing, and thought my sweetest nothings, and looked at the girls and the pleasant gentle sky, and the tall Petri tower with its slender waist, and the calm blue Alster, on which the swans swam, so proud, and beautiful, and secure. The swans! I could look at them for hours — the lovely creatures, with their soft, long necks, as they so voluptuously cradled themselves on the soft flood, diving ever and anon, and proudly splashing till the heaven grew dark and the golden stars came forth yearning, hope-giving, wondrously and beautifully tender and transformed. The stars! Are they golden flowers on the bridal bosom of heaven? Are they the eyes of enamoured angels, who with yearning mirror themselves in the blue streams of earth below and rival with the swans?

Ah! that is all long, long ago. Then I was young and foolish. Now I am old and foolish. Many a flower has withered since that time, and many too been trodden into earth; even the rose-striped stuff of Seligmann has lost the colour warranted to wash. He has faded himself; the firm is now Seligmann's late widow.[1] And Heloise, the gentle creature who seemed to be made to walk only on soft Indian flowered carpets and be fanned with peacock's feathers, went down among roaring

---

1 *Seligmann's selige Witwe*. Seligmann, "happy man," means also a deceased husband. Also a common Jewish name.

sailors, punch, tobacco-smoke, and bad music. "When I again saw Minka she had changed her name to Katinka, and dwelt between Hamburg and Altona; she looked like the temple of Solomon after it had been destroyed by Nebuchadnezzar, and smelt of Assyrian Kanaster; and as she told of Heloise's death, she wept bitterly and tore her hair in despair, and fainted quite away; nor did she recover till she had swallowed a great glass of spirits.

And how the town itself was changed! And the Jungfernstieg! Snow lay on the roofs, and it seemed as if the houses had grown old and had white hair. The lime trees of the Jungfernstieg were dead trees and dry boughs, which waved ghost-like in the cold wind. The sky was cutting blue, and soon grew dark. It was five o'clock on Sunday — the general hour for foddering — and the carriages rolled along. Gentlemen and ladies descended from them with frozen smiles upon their hungry lips. How horrible! At that instant I was thrilled with the awful thought that an unfathomable idiocy appeared in all these faces, and that all persons who passed by seemed bewildered in a strange delirium. Twelve years before, at the same hour, I had seen them with the same faces, like the puppets of a town-hall clock, with the same gestures; and since then they had gone on in the same old way, reckoning and going on 'Change and assisting one another, and moving their jawbones, and paying their *pourboires,* and counting up again: twice two is four. Horrible! I cried. Suppose that it should suddenly occur to one of these people while he sat on the office stool *that twice two is five!* and that he consequently has been multiplying wrongly all his life, and so wasted that life in an awful error. All at once a foolish delirium seized me, and, as I regarded the passers-by more nearly, it seemed to me as if they were themselves nothing but ciphers or Arabic numerals. There went a crook-footed Two by a fatal Three, his full-bosomed, enceinte spouse; behind them came Mr. Four on crutches, waddling along came a fatal Five, then with round belly and a little hood a well-known little Six, and the still better known Evil Seven; but as I looked more closely at the wretched Eight as it tottered past I recognised in it the insurance agent who once went adorned like a carnival ox, but who now looked like the leanest of Pharaoh's lean kine — pale, hollow cheeks, like an empty soup-plate; a cold, red nose, like a winter rose; a shabby black coat, which had a pitiful white shine; a hat into which Saturn with the scythe had cut air-holes; but his boots polished like looking-glasses, and he no longer seemed to think about devouring

Heloise and Minka for breakfast and supper, but to be longing very much more for a good dinner of common beef. And I recognised many an old friend among the mere ciphers who rolled along.

So these and the rest of the numerical folk drove by hurried and hungry, while more grimly droll a funeral passed not far off, past the houses of the Jungfernstieg. As a melancholy, masquerading show there walked on after the hearse, stilted on their little, thin, black silk legs, the well-known council-servants, the privileged civic mourners, in a parodied old Burgundian costume, short black cloaks and black plumped breeches, white wigs, and cravats, out of which the red mercenary faces stared comically, short steel rapiers on their hips, with green umbrellas on their arms.

But more uncanny and bewildering than these figures which went silently by were the sounds which rang in my ears from the other side. They were shrill, harsh, creaking, metallic tones, a crazy screeching, a painful splashing and despairing gulping, a gasping and tumbling, and groaning and wailing bitterly — an indescribable ice-cold cry of pain. The basin of the Alster was frozen up, only that near the shore was a large square cut in the ice, and the terrible tones which I had heard came from the windpipes of the poor white creatures which swam round in it, and screeched in horrible agony; and oh, they were the same swans who once had cheered my heart so softly and merrily. Ah! the beautiful white swans! Their wings had been broken to prevent them from flying in the autumn to the warm South, and now the North held them fast bound, fast banned in its dark, icy grave, and the waiter of the Pavilion said they were all right in there, and that the cold was good for them. But it was not true; it is not good for anybody to be imprisoned, powerless, in a cold pool almost frozen, with the wings broken, so that one cannot fly away to the beautiful South, with its beautiful flowers, golden sunlight, and blue mountain lakes. Ah! with me it was little better, and I understood the suffering of these poor swans, and as it ever grew darker and the stars came out bright above, the same stars who once so warm with love wooed the swans on fair summer nights, but who now looked down with frosty brilliancy, and almost scornfully, on them. Ah! I now perceive that the stars are no living, sympathetic beings, but only gleaming phantasms of night, eternal delusions in a dreamed heaven — mere golden lies in dark blue Nothingness.

CHAPTER V

WHILE writing the foregoing chapter I was thinking all the time on something else. An old song
was humming in my memory, and forms and
thoughts confused themselves most intolerably,
and, willy nilly, I must speak of it. Perhaps it really belongs here, and is right in forcing itself into
my scribbling. Ah, yes! now I begin to understand it, and also to understand the mysterious
tone in which Klas Hinrichson sang it. He was a
Jutlander, and served as our groom. He sang it
the very evening before he hung himself in our
stable. At the refrain—

Sir Vonved, look about thee!

he often laughed bitterly, the horses neighed in
alarm, and the great dog in the courtyard howled
as though some one were dying. It is the old Danish song of Sir Vonved, who rides out into the
world, and adventures about till all his riddles
are answered, and he in vexed mood returns
home. The harp sings in it as refrain from begin-
ning to end. But what did he sing first and last?
I have often thought thereon. Klas Hinrichson's
voice was many a time subdued by tears when
he began the ballad, and then became gradually
as rough and growling as the sea when a storm is
rising. It begins:

Sir Vonved sits in his room alway,
Well on his gold harp he can play;
He hides the gold harp beneath his cloak,
His mother entered, and thus she spoke:
　　"Sir Vonved, look about thee!"

That was his mother Adeline the Queen. She said
to him, "My young son, let others play the harp.
Gird on thy sword, mount thy horse, try thy courage, strive and strain, see the world ere thou turn
again! Sir Vonved, look about thee!"

Sir Vonved binds his sword to his side,
To battle with warriors he will ride;
Strange was his journey and intent,
For no man knew the way he went.
　　Sir Vonved, look about thee!

His helmet was blinking,
His spurs were clinking,
His horse was springing,
In saddle bow swinging!
　　Sir Vonved, look about thee!

He rode one day and then days three,
Yet never a city could he see.
"Ha!" said the youth, "on either hand,
Is there no city in this land?"
　　Sir Vonved, look about thee!

And as he went the road along,
There came to him Sir Thūle Vāng,
Sir Thūle Vāng, with many a son;
They were good warriors every one.
    Sir Vonved, look about thee!

"My youngest son, hear what I say!
Our armour we must change to-day;
My harness must be worn by thee,
Before we fight this hero free."
    Sir Vonved, look about thee!

Sir Vonved draws his sword from his side,
Against the warriors he will ride;
Lord Thūle first of all he slew,
Then all of his twelve sons thereto.
    Sir Vonved, look about thee!

Sir Vonved binds his sword to his side, and rides
on. Then he meets a hunter, and will have half his
game. But the man refuses, and must fight, and is
slain. And

Sir Vonved binds his sword to his side,
And onward ever he will ride;
O'er mountain high, and river deep,
To where a shepherd guards his sheep.
    Sir Vonved, look about thee!

And to the herd as he drew near,
Said, "Whose the flock thou drivest here?
And what is rounder than a wheel?
And where is the merriest Christmas meal?"
    Sir Vonved, look about thee!

"Say where the fish rests in the flood?
And where is the red bird so good?
Where is the best wine made or sold?
Where does Vidrich drink with his
                  warriors bold?"
    Sir Vonved, look about thee!

The herd was silent as could be,
Of all of this no word knew he;
Then at a stroke the herd he slew,
Liver and lung he cleft in two.
    Sir Vonved, look about thee!

Then he came to another flock, and there sat another shepherd, whom he also questioned. This one answers wisely, and Sir Vonved takes a gold ring and puts it on the shepherd's arm. Then he rides further, and comes to Tyge Nold, and slays him with his twelve sons. And, further —

With his horse he rode and ran,
Sir Vonved, the young nobleman,

O'er rocks can ride and rivers swim,
But found no man to talk with him.
  Sir Vonved, look about thee!

He came unto the third, and there
Sat an old man with silver hair:
"List thou, good shepherd, with thy herd,
I deem thou'lt wisely speak a word."
  Sir Vonved, look about thee!

"Oh, what is rounder than a wheel?
Where is the merriest Christmas meal?
Where goes the sun across the sky?
And where do the feet of a dead man lie?"
  Sir Vonved, look about thee!

"What filleth up the valleys all?
What garb is best in royal hall?
What crieth louder than the crane?
And what is whiter than the swan?"
  Sir Vonved, look about thee!

"Who wears his beard on the back, or in?
Who bears his nose beneath his chin?
And what is blacker than a bolt?
Or faster than a frightened colt?"
  Sir Vonved, look about thee!

"Say where the broadest bridge may be,
And what do men most hate to see;
Where is the highest road alone?
And where the coldest drink that's known?"
    Sir Vonved, look about thee!

"The sun is rounder than a wheel,
In heaven the merriest Christmas meal;
The sun forever seeks the west,
Towards east the feet of a dead man rest."
    Sir Vonved, look about thee!

"The snow fills up the valleys all,
Courage beseems a royal hall;
Thunder is louder than the crane,
And angels whiter than the swan."
    Sir Vonved, look about thee!

"The plover's beard on his neck hath grown,
The bear hath his nose 'neath his chin, alone;
Sin is blacker than a bolt,
And thought flies faster than a colt,"
    Sir Vonved, look about thee!

"No broader bridge than ice can be,
The toad is what man most hates to see;
To heaven's the highest road I think,
And in hell they brew the coldest drink."
    Sir Vonved, look about thee!

"Thy answers are as shrewd, I see,
As the questions which I put to thee;
I trust thee well, and will be bound
Thou knowest where heroes may be found."
    Sir Vonved, look about thee!

"The Sonderburg is over there,
Where knights drink mead withouten fear;
There are many kempe and warriors known,
Who well in battle can hold their own."
    Sir Vonved, look about thee!

A golden armlet he unwound,
It weighed, I ween, full fifteen pound;
He placed it in the shepherd's belt,
For showing him where the warriors dwelt.
    Sir Vonved, look about thee!

Then he rode unto the castle, and slew first Randulf and next Strandulf.

He slew strong Ege Under, another,
He slew the Ege Karl his brother;
So right and left his sword blows fall,
To right and left he slew them all.
    Sir Vonved, lock about thee!

Sir Vonved puts his sword in the sheath,
He rides afar o'er the gloomy heath;

In the wild mark he found, ere long,
A warrior, and he was strong.
  Sir Vonved, look about thee!

"Tell me, thou noble rider good,
Where does the fish stay in the flood?
Where is the noblest wine of all?
Where does Vidrich drink with his lords in hall?"
  Sir Vonved, look about thee!

"In the east the fish stays in the flood,
In the north they drink the wine so good;
In Holland thou findest Vidrich alone,
With knights and warriors many a one."
  Sir Vonved, look about thee!

From his breast he took an armlet bright,
And gave it to the other knight:
"Say that thou wert the very last man,
Who ever gold from Sir Vonved wan."
  Sir Vonved, look about thee!

Herr Vonved did to a castle ride,
And bid the porter open wide;
He shut the gate, the bolt he drew,
Over the wall Sir Vonved flew.
  Sir Vonved, look about thee!

His good horse with a rope he bound,
His way to the castle-hall he found;
He sat him at the table free;
Never a word to man spake he.
  Sir Vonved, look about thee!

He ate, he drank, he broke his bread,
Unto the king no word he said:
"Never I heard before a king,
So much accursed chattering!"
  Sir Vonved, look about thee!

The king said to his knights all round,
"The crazy fellow must be bound;
Unless ye bind the stranger tight,
I ween your service is but slight."
  Sir Vonved, look about thee!

"Take five, take twenty, knights, I say,
Come thou thyself into the play;
A whoreson name I give to thee,
Unless by force thou bindest me."
  Sir Vonved, look about thee!

"King Esmer, the father mine,
And my mother, proud Adeline,
Unto me have often told,
With a knave eat not thy gold."
  Sir Vonved, look about thee!

"Was Esmer father then of thine,
And thy mother proud Adeline,
Then thou'rt Vonved, the knight well known,
Also my own dear sister's son."
      Sir Vonved, look about thee!

"Sir Vonved, wilt thou stay with me?
Much honour shall be given thee;
But if away thou will'st to ride,
Many a knight shall go beside."
      Sir Vonved, look .about thee!

"All my gold to thee I give,
If thou here with me 'wilt live."
Sir Vonved would not have it so,
Back to his mother he will go.
      Sir Vonved, look about thee!

Sir Vonved rode along his way,
Grim he was in his soul that day;
Ere he to the castle rode,
Witches twelve before him stood.
      Sir Vonved, look about thee!

With their rock and reel they came before,
And smote him on the knee full sore;
He made his charger leap and spring,
He slew the twelve all in a ring.
      Sir Vonved, look about thee!

He slew the witches as they stood,
From him they got right little good;
He slew his mother with them all,
Cut her in thousand pieces small.
Sir Vonved, look about thee!

In his hall sits Vonved bold,
He drinks the wine so clear and cold;
He played on his gold harp so long,
That all the strings asunder sprang.
Sir Vonved, look about thee![1]

---

1 The Sphynx story appears to have been strangely reproduced in many forms among the Northern races. In the Edda there is a game of questions and answers, ending in the petrifaction of a defeated troll. In the Hervor's Saga, King Heidrek puts riddles to Odin in disguise, and loses his life in consequence of breaking the conditions of the game. Several of the verses of Sir Vonved recall an old English ballad, which is probably of Danish origin: —

"Oh, what is longer than the way?
And what is deeper than the sea?
And what is louder than the horn?
And what is sharper than the thorn?
And what is greener than the grass?
And what is worse than a woman was?"

ANSWER.
"Oh, Love is longer than the way,
And hell is deeper than the sea,
And thunder is louder than the horn,

CHAPTER VI

IT was a charming spring day when I first left Hamburg. I can still see how in the harbour the golden sunrays gleamed on the tarry bellies of the ships, and think I still hear the joyous, long-drawn *Ho-i-ho!* of the sailors. Such a port in spring-time has a pleasant similarity with the feelings of a youth who goes for the first time out into the world on the great ocean of life. All his thoughts are gaily variegated, pride swells every sail of his desires — *ho-i-ho!* But soon a storm rises, the horizon grows dark, the wind's bride[2] howls, the planks crack, the waves break the rudder, and the poor

And hunger sharper than the thorn,
And poison is greener than the grass,
And the devil is worse than a woman was."

When she these questions answered had,
The knight became exceeding glad.

Vonved's mother (a witch) had sent him forth to revenge his father's death. The last verse, which Heine omits, states that he was son of Siegfried the dragon-killer. This ballad made a great impression on George Borrow, who alludes to it in "Lavengro."

2 Wind's bride. The breeze which precedes a tempest.

ship is wrecked on romantic rocks, or stranded on damp, prosaic sandbanks; or perhaps, brittle and broken, with its masts gone, and without an anchor of hope, it returns to its old harbour, and there moulders away, wretchedly unrigged, as a miserable wreck.

But there are men who cannot be compared to common ships, because they are like steamboats. They carry a gloomy fire within, and sail against wind and weather; their smoky banner streams behind, like the black plume of the Wild Huntsman; their zigzagged wheels remind one of weighty spurs with which they prick the ribs of the waves, and the obstinate, resistant element must obey their will like a steed; but sometimes the boiler bursts, and the internal fire burns us up!

But now I will escape from metaphor, and get on board a real ship bound from Hamburg to Amsterdam. It was a Swedish vessel, and besides the hero of these pages, was also loaded with iron, being destined probably to bring as a return freight a cargo of cod-fish to the aristocracy of Hamburg, or owls to Athens.[1]

The banks of the Elbe are charming, especially so behind Altona, near Rainville. There Klopstock lies buried. I know of no place where a dead poet

---

[1] *Stockfische*. Dried cod-fish; also meaning stupid people.

could more fitly rest. To exist there as a *living* poet is, of course, a much more difficult matter. How often have I sought thy grave, oh Singer of the Messiah, thou who hast sung with such touching truthfulness the sufferings of Jesus. But thou didst dwell long enough on the Königstrasse behind the Jungfernstieg to know how prophets are crucified.

On the second day we came to Cuxhaven, which is a colony from Hamburg. The inhabitants are subjects of the Republic, and have a good time of it.[1] When they freeze in winter woollen blankets are sent to them, and when the summer is all too hot they are supplied with lemonade. A high or well-wise senator resides there as pro-consul. He has an income of twenty thousand marks, and rules over five thousand subjects. There is also a sea-bath, which has the great advantage over all others, that it is at the same time an Elbe-bath. A great dam, on which one can walk, leads to Ritze-buttel, which also belongs to Cuxhaven. The term is derived from the Phoenician, as *Ritze* and *Buttel* signify in it the mouth of the Elbe. Many historians maintain that Charlemagne only enlarged Hamburg, but that the Phœnicians founded it about the time that Sodom and Gomorrah were destroyed, and it is not unlikely that fugitives

---

1 *Haben es sehr gut.*

from these cities fled to the mouth of the Elbe. Between the Fuhlentwiete and the coffee factory men have found old money, coined during the reign of Bera XVI. and Byrsa X. I believe that Hamburg is the old Tarsus whence Solomon received whole shiploads of gold, silver, ivory, peacocks, and monkeys. Solomon, that is, the king of Judah and Israel, always had a special fancy for gold and monkeys.

This my first voyage can never be forgotten. My old grand-aunt had told me many tales of the sea, which now rose to new life in my memory. I could sit for hours on the deck recalling the old stories, and when the waves murmured it seemed as if I heard my grand-aunt's voice. And when I closed my eyes I could see her before me, as she twitched her lips and told the legend of the Flying Dutchman.

I should have been glad to see some mermaids, such as sit on white rocks and comb their sea-green hair; but I only heard them singing.

However earnestly I gazed many a time down into the transparent water, I could not behold the sunken cities, in which mortals enchanted into fishy forms lead a deep, a marvellous deep, and hidden ocean life. They say that salmon and old rays[1] sit there, dressed like ladies, at their win-

---

1 *Roche*, the ray or roach.

dows, and, fanning themselves, look down into the street, where cod-fish glide by in trim councillors' costume, and dandy young herrings look up at them through eye-glasses, and crabs, lobsters, and all kinds of such common crustaceans, swarm swimming about. I could never see so deep; I only heard the faint bells of the sunken cities peal once more their old melodious chime.

Once by night I saw a great ship with outspread blood-red sails go by, so that it seemed like a dark giant in a scarlet cloak. Was that the *Flying Dutchman?*

But in Amsterdam, where I soon arrived, I saw the grim Mynheer bodily, and that on the stage. On this occasion, in the theatre of that city, I also had an opportunity to make the acquaintance of one of those fairies whom I had sought in vain in the sea. And to her, as she was particularly charming, I will devote a special chapter.

CHAPTER VII

You certainly know the fable of the *Flying Dutchman.* It is the story of an enchanted ship which can never arrive in port, and which since time immemorial has been sailing about at sea. When it meets a vessel, some of the unearthly sailors

come in a boat and beg the others to take a pack-
et of letters home for them. These letters must
be nailed to the mast, else some misfortune will
happen to the ship—above all if no Bible be on
board, and no horse-shoe nailed to the foremast.
The letters are always addressed to people whom
no one knows, and who have long been dead, so
that some late descendant gets a letter addressed
to a far away great-great-grandmother, who has
slept for centuries in her grave. That timber spectre, that grim grey ship, is so called from the captain, a Hollander, who once swore by all the devils that he would get round a certain mountain,
whose name has escaped me, in spite of a fearful
storm, though he should sail till the Day of Judge-
ment. The devil took him at his word, therefore
he must sail for ever, until set free by a woman's
truth. The devil in his stupidity has no faith in fe-
male truth, and allowed the enchanted captain to
land once in seven years and get married, and so
find opportunities to save his soul. Poor Dutchman! He is often only too glad to be saved from
his marriage and his wife-saviour, and get again
on board.

The play which I saw in Amsterdam was based
on this legend. Another seven years have passed;
the poor Hollander is more weary than ever of his
endless wandering; he lands, becomes intimate

with a Scottish nobleman, to whom he sells diamonds for a mere song, and when he hears that
his customer has a beautiful daughter, he asks that
he may wed her. This bargain also is agreed to.
Next we see the Scottish home; the maiden with
anxious heart; awaits the bridegroom. She often
looks with strange sorrow at a great, time-worn
picture which hangs in the hall, and represents
a handsome man in the Netherlandish-Spanish
garb. It is an old heirloom, and according to a
legend of her grandmother, is a true portrait of
the Flying Dutchman as he was seen in Scotland
a hundred years before, in the time of William of
Orange. And with this has come down a warning
that the women of the family must beware of the
original. This has naturally enough had the result of deeply impressing the features of the picture on the heart of the romantic girl. Therefore,
when the man himself makes his appearance, she
is startled, but not with fear. He too is moved at
beholding the portrait. But when he is informed
whose likeness it is, he with tact and easy con-
versation turns aside all suspicion, jests at the legend, laughs at the Flying Dutchman, the Wandering Jew of the Ocean, and yet, as if moved by the
thought, passed into a pathetic mood, depicting
how terrible the life must be of one condemned
to endure unheard-of tortures on a wild waste

of waters—how his body itself is his living coffin, wherein his soul is terribly imprisoned—how life and death alike reject him, like an empty cask scornfully thrown by the sea on the shore, and as contemptuously repulsed again into the sea—how his agony is as deep as the sea on which he sails—his ship without anchor, and his heart without hope.

I believe that these were nearly the words with which the bridegroom ends. The bride regards him with deep earnestness, casting glances meanwhile at his portrait. It seems as if she had penetrated his secret; and when he afterwards asks, "Katherine, wilt thou be true to me?" she answers, "True to death."

I remember that just then I heard a laugh, and that it came not from the pit but from the gallery of the gods above. As I glanced up I saw a wondrous lovely Eve in Paradise, who looked seductively at me, with great blue eyes. Her arm hung over the gallery, and in her hand she held an apple, or rather an orange. But instead of symbolically dividing it with me, she only metaphorically cast the peel on my head. Was it done intentionally or by accident? That I would know! But when I entered the Paradise to cultivate the acquaintance, I was not a little startled to find a white soft creature, a wonderfully womanly tender being, not languishing, yet delicately clear as crystal, a form of home-like propriety[1] and fascinating amiability. Only that there was something on the left upper lip which curved or twined like the tail of a slippery gliding lizard. It was a mysterious trait, something such as is not found in pure angels, and just as little in mere devils. This expression comes not from evil, but from the *knowledge* of good and evil—it is a smile which has been poisoned or flavoured by tasting the Apple of Eden. When I see this expression on soft, full, rosy, ladies' lips, then I feel in my own a cramp-like twitching—a convulsive yearning—to kiss those lips: it is our Affinity.[2] I whispered into the ear of the beauty:—"*Yuffrou,*[3] I will kiss thy mouth." "*Bei Gott, Mynheer!* that is a good idea," was the hasty answer, which rang with bewitching sound from her heart.

But—no. I will here draw a veil over, and end the story or picture of which the Flying Dutchman was the frame. Thereby will I revenge myself on the prurient prudes who devour such narratives with delight, and are enraptured with them to their heart of hearts, *et plus ultra,* and then abuse the narrator, and turn up their noses at him

---

1 *Ein Bild häuslicher Zucht.*

2 Wahlverwandtschaft. Here better translated by "passional affinity."

3 Yuffrou. Miss, young lady.

in society, and decry him as immoral. It is a nice story, too, delicious as preserved pine-apple or fresh caviare or truffles in Burgundy, and would be pleasant reading after prayers; but out of spite, and to punish old offences, I will suppress it.

Here I make a long dash _____ Which may be supposed to be a black sofa on which we sat as I wooed. But the innocent must suffer with the guilty, and I dare say that many a good soul looks bitterly and reproachfully at me. However, unto these of the better kind I will admit that I was never so wildly kissed as by this Dutch blonde, and that she most triumphantly destroyed the prejudice which I had hitherto held against blue eyes and fair hair. *Now* I understand why an English poet has compared such women to frozen champagne. In the icy crust lies hidden the strongest extract. There is nothing more piquant than the contrast between external cold and the inner fire which, Bacchante-like, flames up and irresistibly intoxicates the happy carouser. Ay, far more than in brunettes does the fire of passion burn in many a sham-calm holy image with golden-glory hair, and blue angel's eyes, and pious lily hands. I knew a blonde of one of the best families in Holland who at times left her beautiful chateau on the Zuyder-Zee and went incognito to Amsterdam, and there in the theatre threw orange-peel on the head of any one who pleased her, and gave herself up to the wildest debauchery, like a Dutch Messalina! ...

When I re-entered the theatre, I came in time to see the last scene of the play, where the wife of the Flying Dutchman on a high cliff wrings her hands in despair, while her unhappy husband is seen on the deck of his unearthly ship, tossing on the waves. He loves her, and will leave her lest she be lost with him, and he tells her all his dreadful destiny, and the cruel curse which hangs above his head. But she cries aloud, "I was ever true to thee, and I know how to be ever true unto death! "

Saying this she throws herself into the waves, and then the enchantment is ended. The Flying Dutchman is saved, and we see the ghostly ship slowly sink into the abyss of the sea.

The moral of the play is that women should never marry a Flying Dutchmen, while we men may learn from it that one can through women go down and perish—under favourable circumstances!

CHAPTER VIII

It was not in Amsterdam alone that the gods were so kind as to take pains to remove my prejudice against blondes. I had opportunities all over Holland to correct my errors in this respect. By my life! I will not exalt the ladies of Holland at the expense of those of other countries — heaven keep me from such injustice! — which would be in me rank ingratitude. Every country has its own kind of women and its own cookery, and in both it is all a matter of taste. One man likes roast chicken, another roast duck; as for me, I love both, and roast goose too.

Regarded from the high idealistic standard, women the world over have a wonderful affinity with the *cuisine* or cookery of their country, wherever it be. Are not British beauties now — candidly confessed — just so wholesome, nourishing, solid, substantial, inartistic, and yet so admirable as old England's good and simple food: roast beef, roast mutton, pudding in flaming cognac, vegetables boiled once in water, with only two kinds of gravy, of which one is melted butter. There smiles no *fricassee*, there we are softly deceived by no flattering *vol-au-vent*, there sighs no refined *ragout*, there we are not flirted with and flattered by a thousand kinds of stuffed, boiled, puffed, roasted, sugared, piquant, sentimental, declamatory, declaratory dishes such as we find in a French restaurant, and which have a startling likeness to all beautiful Frenchwomen. Still we might often observe that by all these the real thing itself is only regarded as a secondary affair, that the roast is not worth so much as the gravy, and that here taste, grace, and elegance are the principal and principle.

Does not the yellow fat, passionately spiced and flavoured, humorously garnished and yet yearning ideal cookery of Italy, express to the life the whole character of Italian beauties? Oh, how I often long for the Lombard *stuffados* and *zampettis,* for the *fegatellis, tagliarinis,* and *broccolis* of blessed Tuscany. All swims in oil, delicate and tender, and trills the sweet melodies of Rossini, and weeps from onion perfume and desire. But macaroni must thou eat with thy fingers, and then it is called — Beatrice!

I often think of Italy, and oftenest by night. The day before yesterday I dreamed that I was there — a checquered Harlequin — and lay all lazy under a weeping willow. The hanging sprays of the tree were of macaroni, which fell, long and lovely, into my mouth, and in between, instead of sunrays, flowed sweet streams of golden butter, and at last a fair white rain of powdered Parmesan.

But from the macaroni of which one dreams no one grows fat — Beatrice!

Not a word about German cookery. It has every virtue and only one fault; and what that is I shall not tell. It has deeply feeling, susceptible pastry without decision, enamoured egg-dishes, admirable steamed dumplings,[1] soul soup with barley,[2] pancakes with apples and pork, virtuous home-forced meat balls and sour cabbage — lucky he who can digest it!

As for the Dutch cookery, it differs from the last, firstly in neatness, secondly by its peculiar relish. The preparation of fish is there indescribably delightful. A perfume of celery, which moves one to the very heart, and is yet deeply intellectual. A self-conscious *naïveté* and garlic.

But when I arrived in Leyden I found the food frightfully bad. The Republic of Hamburg had spoiled me — I must again extol the cookery there, and avail myself of the opportunity to praise the pretty girls and dames of that dear town. Oh, ye divinities! how for the first four weeks did I wish myself back among the smoked-meating houses, the butchers' flesh-world, and the deviltries and

---

1 *Tüchtige Dampfnudeln.*

2 *Gemüthssuppe. Gemüth* is rather one's peculiar disposition or habitual temperament. Pun on *Gemüse,* soft or green vegetables.

the mock turtle-doves of Hammonia! I yearned heart and stomach. If the landlady of the Red Cow had not at last fallen in love with me, I should have died of longing.

Hail to thee, landlady of that Red Cow!

She was a little woman, very plump, with a very little round head. Red little cheeks, little blue eyes, roses and violets. Many an hour we sat side by side in the garden, and drank tea out of real Chinese porcelain cups. It was a beautiful garden, with three and four cornered beds symmetrically strewed with gold sand, cinnabar, and little shining shells. The trunks of the trees were prettily painted red and blue. Copper cages full of canary birds. The most expensive bulbous flowers in variegated and glazed pots. Yew trees charmingly cut into various obelisks, pyramids, vases, and animal forms. Yes, there was a green ox cut from yew, who looked at me jealously when I embraced the lovely landlady of the Red Cow!

Hail to thee, landlady of the Red Cow!

When my frow had covered the upper part of her head with Frisian gold-plates, defended her person with an armour of many-coloured stiff, hard, damask silk, and loaded her arms with the white abundance of her Brabant lace, she looked like a fabulous Chinese puppet—say the goddess of porcelain. And when I, enraptured and inspired, kissed her with a loving smack on both cheeks, she sat in porcelain stillness and sighed porce-languishly,[1] "Mynheer!" — then all the tulips in the garden seemed to feel and wave and sigh in sympathy, "Mynheer!"

This delicate *liaison* procured me many delicacies. For every love-scene of the kind had an influence on the market-basket, which brought provisions to the house and to me. My table companions, six other students, could judge to a nicety by the roast veal or *fillet-de-bœuf* how much I was loved by the landlady of the Red Cow. When the dinner was bad, then the word was, "Just see how miserably Schnabelewopski looks! how yellow and wrinkled his face is; what a cat's melancholy look there is in his eyes, as if they were coming out of his head; why; it's no wonder that our landlady is vexed with him and gives us poor food!" Or else, "Lord help us! Schnabelewopski is growing weaker and feebler every day, and by and by the landlady will love him no more, and then we shall have short commons every day like this; we must feed him up well, so as to make him look nice and plump and rosy." And then they forced all the worst of everything there was on me, and compelled me to eat a great deal

---

1 *Ganz porcellanig.*

of celery.[1] But when we had poor fare for several days in succession, then I was besieged with the most passionate prayers for better provender; to inflame anew the heart of our landlady, to show greater tenderness towards her — in short, to sacrifice myself for the general welfare. It was set before me in long speeches how noble and glorious it was when any one gave himself up heroically for the good of his fellow-citizens, like Regulus, who let himself be put into a spiked barrel, or Theseus, who voluntarily entered the cave of the Minotaur, and then Livy and Plutarch were cited to give examples.

Yes, and I was also pictorially exhorted to rival these examples, by drawing these deeds on the wall, with grotesque variations, for the Minotaur was made to look like the Red Cow on the tavern sign, and the Carthaginian spiked tun like the landlady herself. And those ungrateful youths selected the personal appearance of that excellent woman as a constant butt for their wit. They imitated her round figure with apples, and rolled it up and kneaded its likeness from bread-crumb. They took a large apple for the body, put a little rosy crab-apple on this for the head, and into the former stuck two toothpicks for feet. Or, as I

---

1 Supposed to be an aphrodisiac.

said, they made her from bread-crumb, and then a very little mannikin of the same, which they put on her lap, making the most scandalous remarks. Thus, one said that the smaller figure looked like Hannibal climbing the Alps, while another declared it was more like Marius sitting on the ruins of Carthage. All the same, if I had not climbed those Alps, or seated myself amid those ruins of Carthage, my table companions would have had but sorry fare.

CHAPTER IX

WHEN the food became very bad indeed, then we disputed as to the existence of God. But the beneficent Deity always had the majority. Only three of the table society were atheistically inclined, and even they gave way if we had at least good cheese for dessert. The most zealous Theist was one little Simson,[1] and when he disputed with tall Van Fitter as to whether there was a personal God, he became at times wildly excited, and ran up and down the hall crying constantly, "*Bei Gott!* that isn't fair!"[2] Tall Van Pitter, a lean Frisian, whose

---

1 Simson, *id est* Samson.

2 *Bei Gott, das ist nicht erlaubt.*

soul was as calm as the water in a Dutch canal, and whose words followed one another as leisurely as one canal boat after another, drew his arguments from the German philosophy which was at that time very much studied in Leyden. He ridiculed the narrow-minded men who attribute to God a particular private existence; he even accused them of blasphemy, because they gifted God with wisdom, justice, love, and other human qualities, which are utterly inappropriate, because these are relatively the negations or antitheses of human errors, such as stupidity, injustice, and hate. But when Van Pitter thus developed his own pantheistic views, there came forth against him the fat Fichtean, Dricksen of Utrecht, who stoutly confuted his vague conception of a God spread forth through all Nature — that is to say, existing only in space. Yes, he even declared it was blasphemy to so much us speak of the *existence* of God, since the very idea of existence involved that of space — in short, something substantial. Yes, it was blasphemy even to say of God *He is,* because the purest or most abstract Being[1] could not be conceived without limitations of sense, whereas, if man would think of God, he must abstract Him from all substance, and not

---

1 *Das reinste Sein.*

think of Him as a form of extension, but as a series or order of developments, God not being an action *per se,* but only the principle of a cosmos beyond conception.

Hearing this little Samson fairly raved, and ran up and down the hall, and cried ever more loudly, "O God, O God! By God, that is not fair, O God!" I believe that he would, in honour of God, have beaten the fat Fichtean, had not his arms been too weak; but as it was he often attacked him, when the big and burly one would grasp him by his little arms, hold him fast, and without taking the pipe from his mouth, blow his airy arguments, mixed with tobacco smoke, into Samson's face, so that the little man was almost stifled with fume and fret, and wailed more and more pitifully, "O God! O God!" but it availed him naught, though he defended His cause so valiantly.

Despite this divine indifference, despite this almost human unthankfulness, little Samson remained a staunch champion of Theism, as I believe from inborn inclination; for his father belonged to God's chosen folk, a race which God once very specially protected, and which, in consequence, has maintained till this day a great dependence on him. Jews are ever the most devoted of Deists, especially those who, like little Samson, were born in the vicinity of Frankfort. These may

be as republican as they please in political questions — yes, they may roll in the very mud of *sans
culottéism* — but the instant that religious ideas are
involved they become the humblest servants of
their Jehovah, the old fetish, who, however, will
know nothing of the entire company, and who
has newly baptized himself to a divinely pure
spirit. I believe that this divinely pure spirit, this
new ruler of heaven, who is now conceived as
so moral, so cosmopolite and universal, takes it
ill at heart that the poor Jews, who knew Him in
his rude first form, remind him every day in their
synagogues of his early and obscure national relations. Perhaps the ancient Lord would fain forget
that he was of Palestine origin, and once the God
of Abraham, Isaac, and Jacob, and was in those
times called JEHOVAH.

CHAPTER X

WHILE I lived at Leyden I saw a great deal of little
Samson, and he will be often mentioned in these
memoirs. Next to him I met most frequently another of my table friends, young Van Moeulen. I
could look for hours at his perfectly symmetric
face, thinking what his sister, whom I had never
seen, must be like. All that I knew of her was that

she was said to be the most beautiful woman in Waterland. Van Moeulen was also a beautiful human being, an Apollo, not of marble, but rather of cheese. He was a strange mixture of mind and matter, soul and solid rest. Once in a café he so enraged an Irish gentleman that the latter drew his pistol and fired at him. The ball, however, only knocked the pipe from his mouth; but Van Moeulen's features were as immovable as any Dutchman's head could be, and in the calmest, most indifferent tone, he said, "*Jan, e nüe piep!*" — "John, a fresh pipe!" But his smile was intolerable to me, for then he showed a row of very small white teeth, which looked like a fish spine. Nor did I like it that he wore great gold earrings. He had the strange habit of rearranging every day the furniture in his rooms, and when a visitor came he was generally found putting his bureau where the bed had been, or making the study table change places with the sofa.

Little Samson was in this respect his most painfully earnest antithesis. He could not endure that any one should disturb the least thing in his room; he even became restless and disturbed if one so much as picked up the snuffers. Everything must lay just as it was, for his goods and chattels served him as aids by means of which, according to the principles of mnemonics, he fixed all kinds of historical dates or philosophic principles in his memory. Once when the housemaid carried away from his room an old chest, and removed his shirts and stockings from the bureau for the laundress, he was inconsolable when he returned, declaring that he had lost his whole Assyrian History, and that all his proofs of the immortality of the soul, which he had arranged so systematically in the drawers, were gone to the wash!

Among the originals whom I learned to know in Leyden belongs Mynheer van Bissen, a cousin of Van Moeulen, who introduced him to me. He was professor of theology at the university, and I attended his lectures on the Canticles of Solomon and the Apocalypse of St. John. He was a fine, flourishing, florid man, perhaps of fifty-five, and in his chair was very staid and serious. But once when I called on him and found no one in his study, I saw through the half-opened door of a side-room a very strange sight. This cabinet was furnished in a half-Chinese, half-Pompadour style, with shot-gold[1] damask hangings on the wall, on the ground the most costly Persian carpet, and everywhere marvellous Indian idols, bric-a-brac of mother-of-pearl, flowers, peacock's feathers, and gems, the sofa of red velvet with gold tas-

---

1 *Goldig-schillernde Damasttapeten. Schillern* is to shine while changing colour.

sels; and among it all a raised seat, which looked like a throne, on which sat a little girl, perhaps three years old, clad in a blue satin silver embroidered dress of very antiquated fashion. She held in one hand, like a sceptre, a many-coloured peacock duster, and in the other a faded wreath of laurel. Before her Mynheer ran Bissen was with his little negro page, his poodle, and his monkey, rolling over and over on the ground. They grappled with, tugged and bit one another, while the little girl and a green parrot sitting on its perch cried "Bravo!" At last Mynheer rose from the ground, kneeled before the child, and expressing in a long Latin speech the bravery with which he had fought and conquered his foes, let the little girl crown him with the laurel wreath, while she and the parrot cried "Bravo!" in which I joined as I entered the room.

Mynheer appeared to be somewhat taken aback as I surprised him in his performance. This, I was assured, was his daily amusement; every day he fought and defeated the little negro, the poodle, and the monkey, and was then crowned by the little girl, who was not, however, his own child, but a foundling from the Orphans' Asylum of Amsterdam.

CHAPTER XI

THE house in which I lodged in Leyden was once the dwelling of Jan Steen, the great Jan Steen, whom I regard as being as great as Raphael. And he was even his equal as a *religious* painter. That will be clearly seen when the religion of pain and suffering shall have ended, and the religion of joy tear the mournful veil from the rose-bushes of this earth, and the nightingales at last dare pour forth in rapture their long-suppressed notes of pleasure.

But really no nightingale will ever sing so gaily and rejoicingly as Jan Steen has painted. No one ever felt so deeply that, on this earth, life ought to be one endless Kirmes.[1] He knew that our life is only a coloured kiss of God, and that the Holy Ghost reveals Himself most gloriously in light and laughter.

His eyes looked out into light, and the light mirrored itself in his laughing eyes.

And Jan was always a dear good fellow. "When the harsh old preacher of Leyden sat down on the other side of the fireplace opposite to him, and gave him a long exhortation as to his jovial life, his laughing, un-Christian ways, his drunkenness

---

1 *Kirmess*, or *Kermess*, church mass and an annual festival.

and ill-regulated domestic life and reprobate mer-
riment, Jan listened to him two long hours without betraying the least impatience at this preach-
ing of punishment, until he at last interrupted
him with the words, "Yes, Domine, but the light
would be much better—yes—I beg you, Domine,
just turn your stool a little round to the fire, so
that your face may get a redder tone, while the
rest of the body is in the shadow! "

The Domine rose in a roaring rage and departed, but Jan caught up his palette and painted
the stern old gentleman, just as he had sat in that
punishment-sermon position for model without
knowing it. The picture is admirable, and it hung
in my bedroom in Leyden.

After having seen so many pictures of Jan
Steen in Holland it seems to me as if I knew the
man's whole life. Yes, I knew his whole kith and
kin and acquaintance, wife and children, mother
and cousins all, domestic foes, and other hang-
ers on, absolutely face by face. They salute like
friends from all his pictures, and a collection of
them would be a biography of the painter. He has
often set forth the deepest secrets of his soul with
a few touches of his brush. I am very sure that
his wife often scolded him for drinking, for in his
picture of the Bean Feast, where Jan sits with his
whole family at table, there we see his wife with

a great wine jug in her hand, her eyes gleaming like those of a Bacchante. I am sure, however, that the good woman really drank very little, and the rogue wished to humbug us with the idea that it was his wife and not he who was given to toping. For this cause he himself laughs all the more joyfully from the painting. There he sits, perfectly happy; his son is the Bean-King, and stands on a stool wearing a gilt crown; his old mother, with the happiest wrinkled face, holds the youngest scion in her arms; the musicians play their maddest, merriest dancing melodies, while the ever economical thinking, economically grumbling good wife is set forth to all futurity as if she were tipsy!

How often in my lodgings in Leyden have I thought over the domestic life which this glorious Jan Steen must have experienced and endured. Many a time it seemed that I saw him in the body, sitting at his easel, now and then grasping the great pitcher, "reflecting and drinking, and drinking yet again without reflection." It is not a dreary Catholic spectre, but a modern bright and merry spirit of joyousness, which, now that he is gone, haunts his studio, to paint jolly pictures and drink. Such will be the ghosts whom our descendants will see at times by bright daylight, while the sun shines through the clear white panes; while it is not a black and doleful bell, but scarlet-swelling tones of trumpets, which, pealing from the tower, will announce the pleasant dinner-hour!

The memory of Jan Steen is, however, the best, or rather the only pleasant souvenir of my dwelling in Leyden. Had it not been for that, I should never have held out for eight days in that house. Its exterior was wretched, melancholy, and morbid, or altogether un-Dutch. The dark, mouldy building stood close by the canal, and when one went to the other side it reminded one of an old witch looking at herself in a gleaming magic mirror. As on all Dutch roofs, there always stood on ours a couple of storks. Close by me lodged the cow whose milk I drank every morning, and there was a poultry-roost under my window. My lady-poultry neighbours laid good eggs, but as they always, previous to publishing their works, preceded them by a long and wearisome prospectus of cackling, my enjoyment of their products was materially diminished. Among special annoyances was my landlord's playing the violin all day, and my landlady's playing the devil with him out of jealousy all night.

He who would know all about the mutual relations of this pair needed only to listen to them in a duet. The man performed on the violoncello and his wife on the violin d'amour, but they did not play in time, so that he was always a note behind, and there came withal such cutting cruel tones that when the 'cello growled and the violin gave grinding groans, cue seemed to hear a matrimonial row without words. And after the husband stopped playing, the wife always kept on, as if determined to have the last word. She was a large but very thin women, nothing but skin and bones, a mouth in which false teeth chattered, a low forehead, almost no chin, but a nose which made up for the deficiency, the tip of which curved like a beak, and with which she seemed, when playing, to muffle the sound of a string.

My landlord was about fifty years of age, and had slender legs, a worn away pale face, little green eyes, always blinking like those of a sentinel who has the sun shining in his face. He was by trade a bandage maker, and in religion an Anabaptist. He read the Bible so assiduously that it passed into his nightly dreams, and while his eyes kept winking he told his wife over their coffee how he had again been honoured by converse with holiest dignitaries, how he had even met the highest Holy Jehovah, and how all the ladies of the Old Testament treated him in the friendliest and tenderest manner. This last occurrence was not at all to the liking of my landlady, and she not unfrequently manifested a jealous mood as to these meetings with the blessed damsels of the early days. "If he had only confined his acquaintance, now," she said, "to the pure mother Mary, or old Martha, or, for all I care, even Mary Magdalen, who reformed; but to be meeting night after night those drinking hussies of Lot's daughters, and that precious Mrs. Judith and the vagabond Queen of Sheba, and similar dubious dames, could not be endured." But nothing could equal her rage when one morning her husband gave her an inspired account of how he had enjoyed an interview with the beautiful Esther, who had begged him to help in her toilet when enhancing her charms to fascinate Ahasuerus. In vain did the poor man protest that Mordecai himself had introduced him to his fair ward, that she was quite half-clad, and that his attentions had been confined to combing out her long black hair—the enraged wife beat the poor man with his own bandages, poured hot coffee into his face, and would certainly have made away with him if he had not sworn, in the most solemn manner, in future to avoid all Old Testamental intercourse with ladies, and keep company in future only with the patriarchs and prophets.

The results of this ill-treatment were that from that time Mynheer said nothing about his nightly adventures; he became a religious roué, and confessed to me that he had not only become ultraintimate with the chaste Susanna, but that he had dreamed his way into Solomon's harem, and taken tea with his thousand wives.

CHAPTER XII

"WRETCHED jealousy! Owing to it one of my sweetest dreams—and perhaps the life of little Samson—were brought to a mournful end!

What is dreaming? What is death? Is it only an interruption of life or its full cessation? Yes, for people who only know the Past and the Future, and do not live an eternity in every moment of the Present, death must be terrible! When their two crutches, Space and Time, fall away, then they sink into the eternal Nothing.

And dreams? Why are we not more afraid before going to sleep than to be buried? Is it not terrible that the body can be as if dead all night, while the spirit in us leads the wildest life—a life full of all those terrors of that parting which we have established between life and soul! When in the future both shall be again united in our consciousness, then there will be perhaps no more dreams, or else only invalids, those whose har mony has been disturbed, will dream. The ancients dreamed only softly and seldom; a strong and powerfully impressive dream was for them an event, and it was recorded in their histories.

Real dreaming began with the Jews, the people of the Spirit, and attained its highest development among the Christians, or the spiritual people. Our descendants will shudder when they read what a ghostly life we led, how Humanity was cloven in us and only one half had a real life. Our time — and it begins with the crucifixion of Christ — will be regarded as the great period of illness of Humanity.

And yet, what beautiful sweet dreams we have been able to dream! Our healthy descendants will hardly be able to understand them! All the splendours of the world disappeared from around us, and we found them again *in our own souls;* yes, there the perfume of the trampled roses, and the sweetest songs of the frightened nightingales took refuge.

Thus I feel, and die of the unnatural anxieties and horrible dainties and sweet pains of our time. When I at night undress and lay me in bed, and stretch myself out at full length, and cover myself with the white sheets, I often shudder involuntarily, it seems so like being a corpse and burying myself. Then I close my eyes as quickly as I can to escape this fearful thought, and to save myself in the Land of Dreams.

It was a sweet, kind, sunshiny dream. The heaven was heavenly blue and cloudless, the sea sea-green and still. A boundless horizon; and on the water sailed a gaily-pennoned skiff, and on its deck I sat caressingly at the feet of Jadviga. I read to her strange and dreamy love songs, which I had written on strips of rose-coloured paper, sighing yet joyful, and she listened with incredulous yet inclined ear and deeply-loving smiles, and now and then hastily snatched the leaves from my hand and threw them in the sea. But the beautiful water fairies, with snow-white breasts and arms, rose from the water and caught the fluttering love-lays as they fell. As I bent overboard I could see clearly far down into the depths of the sea, and there sat, as in a social circle, the beautiful water-maids, and among them was a young sprite who, with deeply sympathetic expression, declaimed my love-songs. Wild enraptured applause rang out at every verse; the green-locked beauties applauded so passionately that necks and bosoms grew rosy red, and they praised cordially yet compassionately what they heard. "What strange beings these mortals are! How wonderful their lives, how dire their destinies! They love, and seldom dare express that love; and when they give it utterance at last, they rarely understand one another! And withal they do not lead eternal lives like ours; they are mortal. Only a little time is granted them to seek for happiness, they must grasp it quickly and press it hastily unto their hearts, ere it is gone; therefore their songs of love are so deeply tender, so sweetly painful and anxious, so despairingly gay, such strange blendings of joy and pain. The melancholy shadow of death falls on their happiest hours, and consoles them lovingly in adversity. They can weep. What poetry there is in mortal tears!"

"Dost thou hear," I said to Jadviga, "how they judge of us? Let us embrace, so that they may pity us no longer, and may envy us!" But she the beloved looked at me with infinite love, and without speaking a word. I had kissed her into silence. She grew pale, and a cold shiver thrilled her lovely form. She lay stiff as white marble in my arms, and I had deemed her dead if streams of tears had not poured from her eyes, and these tears flooded me while I held the loved image ever more firmly in my arms.

All at once I heard the keen shrill voice of my landlady, who wakened me from my dream. She stood before my bed with a dark lantern in her hand, and bade me rise quickly and follow her. She absolutely never looked so ugly before!

Without knowing what she wanted, and still half asleep, I went after to where her husband lay, poor man, with night-cap over his eyes, apparently dreaming. He moved his limbs and his lips smiled as if with ineffable happiness, while he rattled and stammered, "Vashti! Queen Vashti! Your Majesty — fear not Ahasuerus — beloved Vashti!"

With eyes glowing with wrath the wife bent over her sleeping spouse, laid her ear to his head as if listening to his thoughts, and whispered to me, "Are you now convinced, Mynheer Schnabelewopski? He has now a love affair with Queen Esther — the scandalous wretch! I found out this horrid intrigue last night. Yes, he has preferred even a heathen to *me*! But I am wife and a Christian, and you shall see how I will revenge myself!"

Saying this she tore away the bedclothes, and grasping a bandage of tough stag leather, laid it on horribly to the poor sinner. He, awakened so unpleasantly from his Biblical dream, screamed out as loudly as if the capital city of Susa were on fire and all Holland under water, and with his shrieks alarmed the whole neighbourhood.

The next day it was all over Leyden that my landlord had raised this cry because he had caught me by night in company with his wife. This latter had been seen half-undressed through the window, and our housemaid who was angry at me, and who had been questioned by the landlady of the Red Lion as to the occurrence, told how she herself had seen Myfrow make a nocturnal visit to my room.

Truly I cannot think of this affair without great pain, and what horrible results there were!

CHAPTER XIII

IF the landlady of the Red Cow had been an Italian she would have poisoned my victuals, but as she was a Dutchwoman she only cooked them as badly as possible. In fact, we experienced the very next day the result of her feminine revenge. The first dish was *no soup*. That was awful, especially for a man brought up decently as I was, who from youth upwards had had soup every day, and who had hitherto never imagined that there was a world where the sun never shone and man soup never knew. The second course was beef, as cold and hard as Myron's cow. Then followed fish, which had indeed an ancient and fish-like smell, and which went untouched in silence as it came. Then came a great, old spectre of a hen, which, far from satisfying our hunger, looked so wretchedly lean and hungry that we, out of sympathetic pity, could not touch it.

"And now, little Samson," cried the burly Dricksen, "dost thou still believe in God? *Is* this just? The Bandage-baggage visits Schnabelewopski in the dark watches of the night, and on that account we must starve by daylight!"

"O God, God!" sighed the little fellow, vilely vexed by such atheistic outbreak, and perhaps by such a miserable meal. And his irritability increased as the tall Van Pitter let fly his arrows of wit against Anthropomorphists and praised the Egyptians who of yore worshipped oxen and onions; the first because they tasted so well when roasted, and the latter when stuffed.

But little Samson under such mockery became furious, and at last he shot forth his defence of Deism.

"God is for man what the sun is for the flowers. When the rays of his heavenly countenance fall on the flowers, then they grow and open out their calyxes, and unfold their most varied colours. By night, when the sun is gone, they stand sorrowful with closed petals, and sleep or dream of the kisses of the golden rays of the past. Those which are ever in the shadow lose colour and growth, shrink and grow pale, and wilt away miserable and unfortunate. But those which grow entirely in the dark, in old castle vaults, under ruined cloisters, become ugly and poisonous; they twine like snakes; their very smell is unhealthy, evilly benumbing, deadly."

"Oh, you need not spin out your Biblical parable any further," said burly Dricksen, as he poured unto himself a great glass of Schiedam gin. "Thou, little Samson, art a pious blossom who inhales in the sunshine of God the holy rays of virtue and love to such inspiration that thy soul blooms like a rainbow, while ours, turned away from God, fade colourless and hideous, if we don't indeed spread forth a poisonous stink."

"I once saw in Frankfort," said little Samson, "a watch which did not believe there was any watchmaker. It was of pinchbeck and went very badly."[1]

"I'll show you anyhow that such a repeater knows how to strike," replied Dricksen, who suddenly became silent and teased Samson no more.

As the latter, notwithstanding his weak little arms, was an admirable fencer, it was determined that the two should duel that day with rapiers. They went at it with great bitterness. The black eyes of little Samson gleamed as if of fire and greatly magnified, and contrasted the more strangely with his little arms, which came forth

---

[1] The famous simile of the watch taken by Paley from Sir Kenelm Digby. *Uhr* in German means both watch and clock.

so pitifully from his rolled-up shirt-sleeves. He became more and more excited; he fought for the existence of God, the old Jehovah, the King of kings. But He aided not in the least His champion, and in the sixth round the little man got a thrust in the lungs.

"O God!" he cried, and fell to the ground.

CHAPTER XIV

THIS scene excited me terribly. But all the fury of my feelings turned against the woman who had directly caused such disaster, and with a heart full of wrath and pain I stormed into the Red Cow.

"Monster, why did you not serve us soup?" These were the words with which I addressed the landlady, who became deadly pale as I entered the kitchen. The porcelain on the chimney-piece trembled at the tone of my voice. I was as desperate as only that man can be who has had no soup, and whose best friend has just had a rapier through his lungs.

"Monster, why did you not serve us soup?" I repeated these words, while the consciously guilty woman stood as if frozen and speechless before me. But at last, as if from opened sluices, the tears poured from her eyes. They flooded her whole face, and ran down into the canal of her bosom. But this sight did not soften me, and with still greater bitterness I cried, "O ye women, I know that ye can weep, but are tears *soup?* Ye are created for our misery. Your looks are lies, and your breath is treason and deceit. Who first ate the apple of sin? Geese saved the Capitol, but a woman ruined Troy. O Troy, Troy! thou holy fortress of Priam, thou didst fall by a woman! Who cast Marcus Aurelius into destruction? By whom was Marcus Tullius Cicero murdered? Who demanded the head of John the Baptist? Who was the cause of Abelard's mutilation? A woman. History is replete, yea unto repletion, with the terrible examples of man's ruin caused by you. All your deeds are folly, and all your thoughts are ingratitude. We give you the highest, the holiest flame of our hearts, our love—and what do we get for it? Beef that the devil would not eat, and worse poultry. Wretch and monster, why did you serve no soup?"

Myfrow began to stammer a series of excuses, and conjured me, by all the sweet memories of our love, to forgive her. She promised to provide better provender than before, and only charge six florins per head, though the Groote Dohlen landlord asked eight for his ordinary. She went so far as to promise oyster patties for the next day—

yes, in the soft tone of her voice there was even a perfume as of truffles. But I remained firm. I was determined to break with her for ever, and left the kitchen with the tragic words, "Farewell; between us two all is cooked out forever!"

In leaving I heard something fall. Was it a pot for cooking or Myfrow herself? I did not take the pains to look, and went straight to the Groote Dohlen to order six covers for the next day.

After this important business I hurried to little Samson's house and found him in evil case. He lay in an immense old-fashioned bed which had no curtains, and at the corners of which were great marbled wooden pillars which bore above a richly gilt canopy. The face of the little fellow was pale from pain, and in the glance which he cast at me was so much grief, kindness, and wretchedness, that I was touched to the heart. The doctor had just left him, saying that his wound was serious. Van Moeulen, who alone had remained to watch all night, sat before his bed, and was reading to him from the Bible.

"Schnabelewopski," sighed the sufferer, "it is good that you came. You may listen, and 'twill do you good. That is a dear, good book. My ancestors bore it all over the world with them, and much pain, misfortune, cursing and hatred, yes, death itself, did they endure for it. Every leaf in it cost tears and blood: it is the written fatherland of the children of God; it is the holy inheritance of Jehovah."

"Don't talk so much; it's bad for you," said Van Moeulen.

"And indeed," I added, "don't talk of Jehovah, the most ungrateful of gods, for whose existence you have fought to-day."

"O God!" sighed the little man, and tears fell from his eyes, "Thou help'st our enemies,"

"Don't talk so much," said Van Moeulen again. "And thou, Schnabelewopski," he whispered to me, "excuse me if I bore thee; the little man would have it that I should read to him the history of his namesake Samson. We are at the fourteenth chapter — listen!

"'Samson went down to Timnath, and saw a woman in Timnath of the daughters of the Philistines.'"

"No," said the patient with closed eyes, "we are at the sixteenth chapter. It is to me as if I were living in all that which you read me, as if I heard the sheep bleating as they feed by Jordan, as if I myself had set fire to the tails of the foxes and chased them through the fields of the Philistines, and as if I had slain a thousand Philistines with the jawbone of an ass. Oh the Philistines! they enslaved and mocked us, and made us pay toll like swine, and slung me out of doors from the ball-room on the Horse, and kicked me at Bocken-heim — kicked me out of doors from the Horse! — oh, by God, that was not fair."

"He is feverish, and has wild fancies," softly said Van Moeulen, and began the sixteenth chapter.

"'Then went Samson to Gaza, and saw there an harlot, and went in unto her.

"'And it was told the Gazites, saying, Samson is come hither. And they compassed him in, and laid wait for him all night in the gate of the city, and were quiet all the night, saying, In the morning, when it is day, we shall kill him.

"'And Samson lay till midnight, and arose at midnight, and took the doors of the gate of the city, and the two posts, and went away with them, bar and all, and put them upon his shoulders, and carried them up to the top of an hill that is before Hebron.

"'And it came to pass afterward, that he loved a woman in the valley of Sorek whose name was Delilah.

"'And the lords of the Philistines came up unto her and said unto her, Entice him and see wherein his great strength lieth, and by what means we may prevail against him, that we may bind him to afflict him: and we will give thee every one of us eleven hundred pieces of silver.

"'And Delilah said to Samson, Tell me, I pray thee, wherein thy great strength lieth, and wherewith thou mightest be bound to afflict thee.

"'And Samson said unto her, If they bind me with seven green withes that were never dried, then shall I be weak and be as another man.

"'Then the lords of the Philistines brought up to her seven green withs which had not been dried, and she bound him with them.

"'Now there were men lying in wait, abiding with her in the chamber. And she said, The Philistines be upon thee, Samson. And he brake the withs, as a thread of tow is broken when it toucheth the fire. So his strength was not known.'"

"Oh, the fools of Philistines!" cried the little man, and smiled well pleased; "and they wanted to take me up and put me in the constable's guard."

Van Moeulen read on: —

"'And Delilah said to Samson, Behold, thou hast mocked me, and told me lies: now tell me, I pray thee, wherewith thou mightest be bound.

"'And he said unto her, If they bind me fast with new ropes that never were occupied, then shall I be weak, and be as another man.

"'Delilah therefore took new ropes, and bound him therewith, and said unto him, The Philistines be upon thee, Samson. And there were liers in wait abiding in the chamber. And he brake them from off his arms like a thread.'"

"Fools of Philistines," cried the little man.

"'And Delilah said unto Samson, Hitherto thou hast mocked me, and told me lies: tell me wherewith thou mightest be bound? And he said unto her, If thou weavest the seven locks of my head with the web.

"'And she fastened it with the pin, and said unto him, The Philistines be upon thee, Samson. And he awaked out of his sleep, and went away with the pin of the beam, and with the web.'"

The little man laughed. "That was in the Eschenheimer Lane." But Van Moeulen continued: —

"'And she said unto him, How canst thou say, I love thee, when thine heart is not with me? Thou hast mocked me these three times, and hast not told me wherein thy great strength lieth.

"'And it came to pass, when she pressed him daily with her words, and urged him, so that his soul was vexed unto death;

"'That he told her all his heart, and said unto her, There hath not come a razor upon mine head; for I have been a Nazarite unto God from my mother's womb; if I be shaven, then my strength will go from me, and I shall become weak, and be like any other man.'"

"What folly!" sighed the little man. Van Moeulen kept on: —

"'And when Delilah saw that he had told her all his heart, she sent and called for the lords of the Philistines, saying, Come up this once, for he hath showed me all his heart. Then the lords of the Philistines came up unto her and brought money in their hand.

"'And she made him sleep upon her knees, and she called for a man and caused him to shave off the seven locks of his head; and she began to afflict him, and his strength went from him.

"'And she said, The Philistines be upon thee, Samson. And he awoke out of his sleep, and said, I will go out as at other times before, and shake myself. And he wist not that the Lord was departed from him.

"'But the Philistines took him, and put out his eyes, and brought him down to Gaza, and bound him with fetters of brass; and he did grind in the prison house.'"

"O God! God!" wailed and wept the sick man. "Be quiet!" said Van Moeulen, and read on: —

"'Howbeit the hair of his head began to grow again after he was shaven.

"'Then the lords of the Philistines gathered them together for to offer a great sacrifice unto Dagon their god, and to rejoice: for they said, Our God hath delivered Samson our enemy into our hand.

"'And when the people saw him, they praised their god: for they said, Our God hath delivered into our hands our enemy, and the destroyer of our country, which slew many of us.

"'And it came to pass, when their hearts were merry, that they said, Call for Samson, that he may make us sport: and they called for Samson out of the prison house; and he made them sport: and they set him between the pillars.

"'And Samson said unto the lad that held him by the hand, Suffer me that I may feel the pillars whereupon the house standeth, that I may lean upon them.

"'Now the house was full of men and women; and all the lords of the Philistines were there; and there were upon the roof about three thousand men and women, that beheld while Samson made sport.

"'And Samson called unto the Lord, and said, O Lord God, remember me, I pray thee, and strengthen me, I pray thee, only this once, O God, that I may be at once avenged of the Philistines for my two eyes.

"'And Samson took hold of the two middle pillars upon which the house stood, and on which it was borne up, of the one with his right hand, and of the other with his left.

"'And Samson said, Let me die with the Philistines. And he bowed himself with all his might; and the house fell upon the lords, and upon all the people that were therein. So the dead which he slew at his death were more than they which he slew in his life.'"

At this little Samson opened his eyes spectrally wide, raised himself spasmodically, seized with his slender arms the two pillars at the foot of his bed, and shook them, crying out in wrath, "Let me die with the Philistines!" The strong columns remained immovable; but, exhausted and smiling sadly, the little man fell back on his pillow, while from his wound, the bandage of which was displaced, ran a red stream of blood.

Books published by Mondial

French Classics:

1. Rougon-Macquart Series:

Emile Zola: The Fortune of the Rougons
ISBN 1595690107 / 9781595690104

Emile Zola: The Fat and the Thin
(The Belly of Paris)
ISBN 1595690522 / 9781595690524

Emile Zola: Abbe Mouret's Transgression
(The Sin of the Abbé Mouret)
ISBN 1595690506 / 9781595690500

Emile Zola: The Dream
ISBN 1595690492 / 9781595690494

Emile Zola: A Love Episode (A Page of Love)
ISBN 1595690271 / 9781595690272

Emile Zola: The Conquest of Plassans
ISBN 1595690484 / 9781595690487

Emile Zola: The Joy of Life (Zest for Life)
ISBN 1595690476 / ISBN 9781595690470

Emile Zola: Doctor Pascal
ISBN 1595690514 / 9781595690517

Emile Zola: His Excellency
(His Excellency, Eugène Rougon)
ISBN 1595690557 / 9781595690555

Emile Zola: Money
ISBN 9781595690630

Emile Zola: The Soil (The Earth)
ISBN 9781595690883

2. Other French Literature:

Emile Zola: The Mysteries of Marseille
ISBN 9781595690913

Emile Zola: The Flood. ISBN 9781595690944

Emile Zola: Death. ISBN 9781595690937

Emile Zola: Fruitfulness (The Four Gospels)
ISBN 1595690182 / 9781595690180

Emile Zola: The Fête in Coqueville
(The Coqueville Spree) ISBN 9781595690869

Victor Hugo: Ninety-Three. ISBN 9781595690920

Victor Hugo: Bug-Jargal. ISBN 9781595690951

Victor Hugo: The Man Who Laughs
(By Order of the King)
ISBN 1595690131 / 9781595690135

Victor Hugo: History of a Crime
ISBN 1595690204 / 9781595690203

Voltaire: The Princess of Babylon
ISBN 9781595690999

Honoré de Balzac: Ursula (Ursule Mirouet)
ISBN 1595690530 / 9781595690531

Honoré de Balzac: Maitre Cornelius
ISBN 1595690174 / 9781595690173

Anatole France: Penguin Island
ISBN 1595690298 / 9781595690296

Anatole France: The Crime of Sylvestre Bonnard
ISBN 9781595690593

Gustave Flaubert: Salammbo (Salambo)
ISBN 1595690352 / 9781595690357

Romain Rolland: Pierre and Luce
ISBN 9781595690609

Jules Verne: An Antarctic Mystery
(The Sphinx of the Ice Fields)
ISBN 1595690549 / 9781595690548

André Gide: Strait is the Gate
(La Porte étroite) ISBN 9781595690623

André Gide: Prometheus Illbound
ISBN 9781595690807

André Gide: Recollections of Oscar Wilde.
ISBN 9781595690814

German Classics:

Heinrich Heine: Germany. A Winter Tale
(Deutschland. Ein Wintermärchen.)
Bilingual Edition. ISBN 9781595690715

Heinrich Heine: The Rabbi of Bacharach
(German Classics) ISBN 9781595691002

Heinrich Heine: Florentine Nights.
(German Classics) ISBN 9781595691019

Johann Wolfgang von Goethe:
The Sorrows of Young Werther
ISBN 159569045X / 9781595690456

Theodor Storm: The Rider of the White Horse
(The Dykemaster) ISBN 9781595690746

Heinrich von Kleist: Michael Kohlhaas
(A Tale from an Old Chronicle)
ISBN 9781595690760

Gottfried Keller: A Village Romeo and Juliet
(Swiss-German Classics) ISBN 9781595690791

Gottfried Keller: Ursula
(Swiss-German Classics) ISBN 9781595690838

Gottfried Keller: The Governor of Greifensee
(Swiss-German Classics) ISBN 9781595690845

Wilhelm Raabe: The Hunger Pastor
(German Classics) ISBN 9781595690753

**Theodor Storm, Adelbert von Chamisso,
Adalbert Stifter:** Famous German Novellas of the
19th Century (Immensee. Peter Schlemihl. Brigitta.)
ISBN 159569014X / 9781595690142

Other books:

Agatha Christie: Two Novels (The Mysterious
Affair at Styles. The Secret Adversary.)
ISBN 1595690417 / 9781595690418

Jack London: War of the Classes. Revolution.
The Shrinkage of the Planet.
ISBN 1595690409 / 9781595690401

Jack London: Before Adam. Children of the Frost.
ISBN 1595690395 / 9781595690395

Jack London: The Iron Heel
ISBN 1595690379 / 9781595690371

Oscar Wilde: The Critic as Artist. Upon the Importance of Doing Nothing and Discussing Everything. ISBN 9781595690821

Oscar Wilde, Anonymous: Teleny or The Reverse of the Medal (Gay erotic classic) ISBN 1595690360 / 9781595690364

Martin Andersen Nexo: Pelle the Conqueror (Complete Edition: Boyhood. Apprenticeship. The Great Struggle. Daybreak.) ISBN 159569028X / 9781595690289

Martin Andersen Nexo: Ditte Everywoman (Complete Edition: Girl Alive. Daughter of Man. Towards the Stars.) ISBN 9781595690333

Susan Coolidge: Clover ISBN 1595690263 / 9781595690265

Jerome K. Jerome: Idle Thoughts of an Idle Fellow ISBN 1595690247 / 9781595690241

Malama Katulwende: Bitterness
(An African Novel from Zambia)
ISBN 159569031X / 9781595690319

Sigmund Freud: Dream Psychology
(Psychoanalysis for Beginners)
ISBN 1595690166 / 9781595690166

Gertrude Stein: Three Lives
(With an Introduction by Carl Van Vechten)
ISBN 1595690425 / 9781595690425

Gabriele D'Annunzio:
The Child of Pleasure. ISBN 9781595690581

Carl Van Vechten: Firecrackers.
A Realistic Novel. ISBN 9781595690685

Bruce Kellner: Winter Ridge. A Love Story.
ISBN 9781595690692

Donald Windham: Two People
ISBN 9781595691033

Frederick (Friedrich) Engels: Socialism: Utopian and Scientific (Appendix: The Mark; Preface by Karl Marx) ISBN 1595690468 / 9781595690463

Karl Marx: The Eighteenth Brumaire of Louis Bonaparte. ISBN 1595690239 / 9781595690234